This Little Tiger
book belongs to:

_____

_____

For Kate and Anna
E. B.

For Louise,
from Greg!

LITTLE TIGER PRESS
An imprint of Magi Publications
1 The Coda Centre, 189 Munster Road,
London SW6 6AW
www.littletigerpress.com

First published in Great Britain 2005
This edition published 2006

Text copyright © Elizabeth Baguley 2005
Illustrations copyright © Magi Publications 2005
Elizabeth Baguley has asserted her right to be
identified as the author of this work under the
Copyright, Designs and Patents Act, 1988

A CIP catalogue record for this book is available
from the British Library

Printed in Singapore by Tien Wah Press Pte.

2 4 6 8 10 9 7 5 3 1

MEGGIE MOON

ELIZABETH BAGULEY

illustrated by
GREGOIRE MABIRE

LITTLE TIGER PRESS
London

Digger and Tiger spent all their time in the Yard. Nothing grew there but piles of dented things, empty things, worn-out things. No one else dared come to the Yard. It was *their* place.

Digger and Tiger were
rough-and-tumble boys,
spiky-haired, hole-at-the-knee boys.
They were not brothers, but they went
together like a dustbin and its lid.

One day a girl arrived.
She walked through the
high gate and clicked it
shut behind her. She stared
at the tangled rubble and
the king-of-the-castle boys.
The boys stared back.

"I'm Meggie Moon," said
the girl. "Can I play with
you?"

"We don't play with
girls," snarled Tiger.

"Girls don't know how
to play," hissed Digger.

"Oh, don't they?" said
Meggie, laughing.

Meggie left the boys standing in the shadows and went to explore. The Yard was a mess and the boys were unfriendly, but Meggie had ideas.

She picked up some of the
rubbish and began
to arrange it . . .

a tin here and
a pipe there . . .

until . . .

"It's a racing car!" said Tiger.
"You can drive it if you want," offered Meggie.
"Not likely," said Digger.

But as soon as Meggie left,
the boys jumped into the car
and raced away until dark.

The next day Meggie
came to the Yard again.
Digger and Tiger watched
her picking over the junk.
 "Go on, then, build
something!" ordered Tiger.
 So Meggie made a ship.
When it was finished,
the boys played pirates.
 "Can I come aboard?"
she asked.
 "I suppose you
could be our cook,"
said Tiger.

"I'd rather be your lookout," said Meggie.
She spat on her hands, shot up the
rigging and shouted, "Enemy ship ahoy!"
Startled, the boys drew their cutlasses.
"Aye-aye, shipmate!" they said.

By the third day the car was mangled and the ship wrecked.

"Let's kick cans," said Tiger.

"I'd rather throw stones," whinged Digger.

"That's boring," said Meggie. "Why don't we make a den?"

She found wall-things and roof-things and the boys crammed and jammed them into a corner. They played until dark, when the bed calls came.

Every day Meggie
thought of something
different. They crossed
a snake pit, shivered
through a haunted
castle, lurched round
a roller-coaster . . .
 "She's not bad – for a
girl," Digger admitted
to Tiger, secretly.

Then, one day, Meggie announced,
"I'm going home tomorrow."
    The boys gazed at the Yard.
They remembered how, before Meggie
came, the rubble was just rubble.
    "But what shall we play?"
wailed Digger.

"I've brought you a goodbye present.
You can play with that."
    Meggie wheeled in a towering
load and toppled it in
front of them.

"Star troops at the
ready!" she commanded,
then marched out through
the gate, clicking it shut
behind her.

"Aye-aye, Captain," Digger and
Tiger saluted, but Meggie had gone.
The sound of the closing gate
echoed through the Yard.

The boys stared emptily after
Meggie. At last they inched towards
her present-pile. The heap of rubble
was just . . . a porthole here,
a jet there . . .
   The boys looked at each other.
They had ideas.

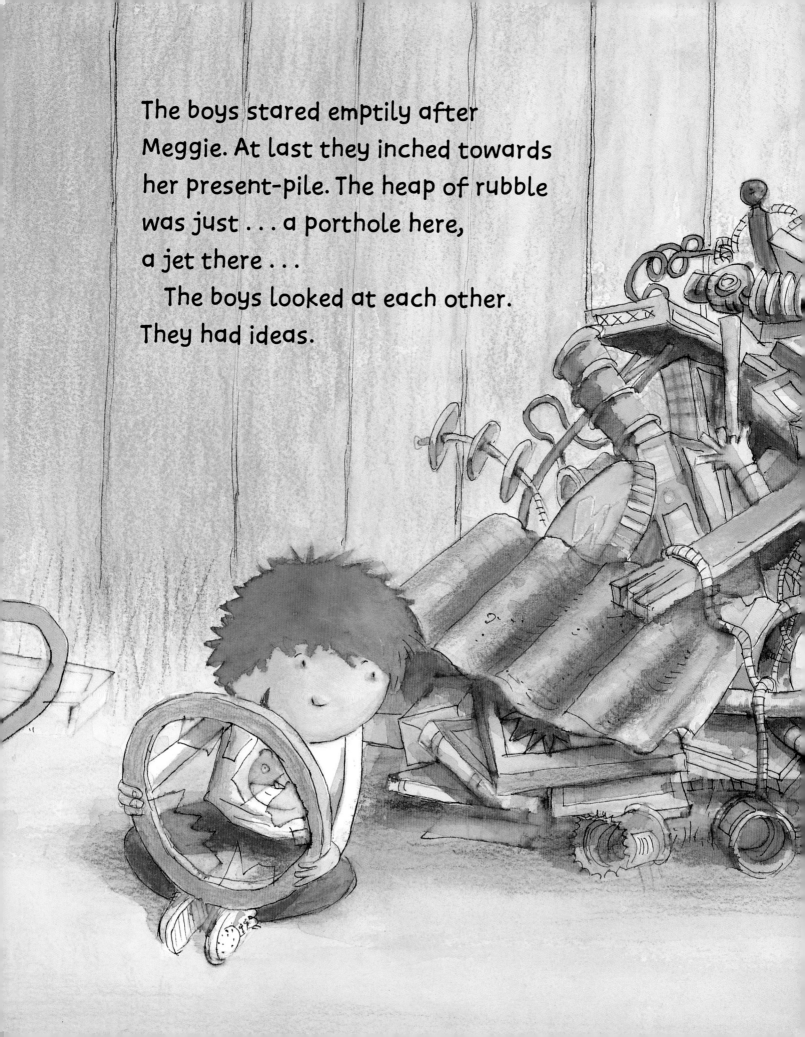

"Star troops!" barked Digger.
"At the ready!" shouted Tiger.

By dusk, smooth
things and crumpled
things . . .

shattered things and
battered things . . .

spiralled high
above the Yard
fence.

With spacesuits on, the astronauts climbed into the rocket. "...!" they chorused. With ... a rumble, the rocket burst ... life and Digger and Tiger shot ... skywards – away, away from the Yard in the Starship Meggie Moon.

Books to give you brilliant ideas from Little Tiger Press

At the End of the
Rainbow
A H Benjamin & John Bendall-Brunello

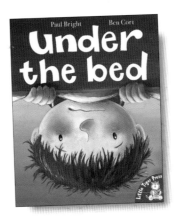
POOH!
IS THAT YOU, BERTIE?
David Roberts

Paul Bright   Ben Cort
Under the bed

Foley
and
Jem
Mary Murphy   Mark Oliver

Too Busy for Benjie
Christine Leeson
Andy Ellis

Nobody Laughs at a Lion!
Paul Bright   Illustrated by Matt Buckingham

For information regarding any of the above titles or
for our catalogue, please contact us:
Little Tiger Press, 1 The Coda Centre,
189 Munster Road, London SW6 6AW
Tel: 020 7385 6333 Fax: 020 7385 7333
E-mail: info@littletiger.co.uk
www.littletigerpress.com